# Romeo and Juliet

*Written by*
Jon Mayhew

*Illustrated by*
Barbara Vagnozzi

**Collins**

# Cast of characters

Romeo Montague

Lord Montague

Lady Montague

the Prince

Mercutio

Benvolio

Balthasar

Juliet Capulet

Lord Capulet

Lady Capulet

Paris

Tybalt

the Nurse

Friar Laurence

3

# Prologue

My name is Balthasar, loyal servant and friend to
Romeo Montague. I grew up with him – my family have
served the Montagues for generations. We were like brothers
in some ways but I always knew he was my master. I should've
protected him but everything has gone wrong and it's all
my fault.

I was there at the start of all the troubles and I should've
stopped it when I could. I was the one who delivered the fateful
message when I should've known what my master would do.

I was the one who could've saved him. But I didn't.

# 1 Riot!

Verona was a beautiful town full of narrow cobbled streets and peaceful squares with tinkling fountains. But the town also held a darkness. A hatred that grew over the centuries. Two rich families lived in Verona, the Montagues and the Capulets. They despised each other. They always had. Something happened a long time ago. Nobody can even remember what it was but the two sides have never forgiven each other. That means their servants too. My family's worked for the Montagues for so long, in a way we're part of their family. If they hate the Capulets, then we do too!

My story starts with a fight in Verona's town square.
I remember that day so well. The heat was unbearable.
The sun beat down on the shoppers in the market, making
them feel sticky and uncomfortable. Everyone was in a foul
mood. People grumbled about prices and accused the market
stall-holders of trying to cheat them. Many townsfolk stayed in
the shade of their homes, keeping the shutters tightly closed.

I heaved the basket of fruit that my friend Abraham and I had
just bought on to my back as if it were a sack of boulders. Sweat
had already begun to trickle down my back. I squinted across
the town square, the sunlight dazzling me.

"Oh no, that's all we need," I muttered.

Sampson and Gregory, two servants from the House of Capulet, came stamping across the cobbles towards us, obviously eager for trouble. Their red uniforms made them look angry in the hot town square.

"This'll be the third time they've tried to pick a fight," Abraham muttered to me. "And I'm in the mood to have one!"

"Just ignore them," I pleaded. "We've got to get back to the cook with these groceries."

It was too late, though. Gregory came strolling across to us, giving us a funny look, and that's all Abraham needed.

"What are you looking at?" he asked.

Gregory gave Abraham a contemptuous look. "Not much," he sneered.

"My Lord Montague is a better man than your Capulet!"
Abraham growled, his knuckles whitening as he gripped his
grocery basket tightly.

"If you want a fight, then you've got one!" Gregory yelled,
drawing his blade. "Nobody insults the Capulets!"

I leapt back as Sampson drew his sword too.
Abraham drew also.

"Stop it, now!" I shouted but it had gone too far. Tempers were frayed and the heat had got the better of them. Somebody pushed a market stall over. People started screaming.

More servants from the Capulets' house poured into the square and then more Montague servants. Lord Montague, Romeo's father, appeared, waving a sword. Lady Montague was trying to drag him back. "Stop, my dear!" she screamed at him. "You're too old for this. You'll get hurt!"

"Stand by while the Capulets attack my servants and make fun of the name of Montague? Never!" Lord Montague yelled.

On the other side of the square, I think I saw Lord Capulet shouting something similar. It was a full-scale riot.

I hid behind a barrel and curled into a ball, hoping nobody would find me where I was hiding. I didn't want to be attacked by any Capulets but I didn't want any Montagues to see me and accuse me of being a coward, either.

From my hiding place I heard a trumpet sound. It was the Prince, the ruler of the whole town. He came galloping into the square, dressed in fine silks and velvets. His cloak billowed behind him as his horse barged folk aside. His guards charged alongside him, knocking over anyone stupid enough to get in the way.

The Prince bellowed from on top of his snorting white horse. "Rebellious subjects, throw your weapons to the ground!"

The sound of metal hitting the ground echoed all over the market square. I crept from my hiding place to listen to what the Prince had to say. His word was law and I knew he was losing patience with us all.

The Prince scanned the crowd, people panting for breath and nursing swollen eyes, cuts and bruises. "I'm tired of trying to stop these petty squabbles," he roared. "If anyone starts a disturbance like this again, they'll pay for it with their lives! Now, on pain of death, all men depart!"

People didn't need telling twice. They hurried away, gathering up anything they'd dropped as quickly as they could. The Montagues and the Capulets went back to their houses.

Abraham staggered out of the crowd towards me. He looked terrible. His eye was closed up with a huge bruise and his arm hung limply by his side. He glared at me. If only I could've stopped that first fight, then the Prince wouldn't have made his ruling. And maybe the fatal chain of events might never have started.

# 2 Forebodings

Romeo hadn't been involved in the fighting. I found him wandering the streets with his friends. They were all laughing and acting the fool but Romeo looked serious. He's a bit of a dreamer, and his friends were making fun of him.

"Where have you been, Balthasar?" he asked, as I approached.

I shook my head and shrugged. "Tidying up at the house, sir," I said. "There was a terrible fight with the Capulets. Only the Prince could stop it in the end."

"People should think more about love than hate," Romeo sighed.

I laughed. "You're always in love, sir," I said, winking at him. "How old are you? Sixteen? There's plenty of time. You just haven't found the right girl yet!"

It was true. He was a handsome young man and the Montagues were a rich family but the girls he fell for didn't usually think much of him.

"Well, all that'll change tonight!" Mercutio, one of Romeo's friends, said. Mercutio was a bit older than Romeo and a cousin of the Prince's. I didn't like him. He was always mocking people and I thought he was a bad influence on Romeo, always trying to get him to do things he shouldn't. He ignored me, a mere servant. Mercutio grinned. "We're going to the Capulets' ball!"

Everyone knew that Lord Capulet threw the best parties and one of them was happening tonight. Everyone was invited. Everyone except the Montagues, of course.

13

I frowned. "Isn't that a bit dangerous, sir?" I asked Romeo.

"Possibly," Romeo said, faintly. "Maybe I shouldn't go."

Mercutio gave a snort and slapped Romeo on the back. "Oh, come on!" he said. "You can't back out now – Benvolio and all the others are going, so you'll have to come too!"

"But they'll recognise you, sir!" I gasped.

"Nonsense! It's a masked ball," Mercutio said, still looking at Romeo as if he'd spoken and not me. "Nobody will know who we are."

Soon Benvolio and all Romeo's other friends were surrounding him, cheering, singing and pulling their masks on. I didn't think they made very good disguises. I stood on the edge of the crowd, watching them laughing and pointing at each other in their masks.

Darkness fell over the town and the evening felt a little cooler. I followed Romeo. Mercutio kept slapping him on the back and pushing him along.

I had a real sense that something terrible was going to happen because of the party. No good could come of it, I thought, Montagues gatecrashing a Capulet party. Things could get nasty.

How I wish I'd tried to persuade my master to stay away, to go home and not get involved. But I was just a servant, and Romeo's friends were almost dragging him along.

# 3 The party

The Capulets' house was as impressive as the Montagues',
I had to admit. It had a courtyard in the centre of it, with
fountains and cool marble tiles. An orchard grew around
the house, full of big, old orange, lemon and olive trees.
Fruit and bread littered the tables. The smell of roast chicken,
venison and beef hung in the air, making my mouth water.

Romeo turned to me and handed me a mask. "Wear this
and follow me in," he said. "Keep an eye out for any Capulets
who might recognise us. Keep to the shadows."

I slipped into the side of the room, hiding by a big stone pillar
as Romeo commanded. I could see everything. Servants rushed
around, trying to keep everyone supplied with drinks and food
while musicians played for the gentlefolk to dance.

Torches flickered all around the hall and I began to relax. The light was quite bad and, if he kept his mask on, Romeo might keep out of trouble. There were all kinds of important people there. The Prince didn't attend but Paris, his cousin was there. Paris was a rich, handsome man and rumour had it that he was on the lookout for a wife. Women flocked around him, smiling and curtsying, desperate to catch his eye.

I also saw many hated Capulets. What was Romeo thinking, coming to this party? Tybalt Capulet stood, arms folded, watching everyone dance. A nephew to Lord Capulet, he was a villain if ever there was one! He was tall and dark-haired, with a cruel face. He loved fighting, especially with swords. He'd hurt a lot of people during the riot that morning.

I leant against the pillar and started to doze, the hot day and all the excitement finally getting to me, when I noticed Romeo freeze to the spot and stare. He looked like he'd been turned to stone. He was staring at a girl.

"Oh no," I groaned. I could tell that he was hypnotised by her. "He's in love again!"

Romeo dashed over and took the girl's hand; they joined the dancing and began to talk. She seemed as bewitched by Romeo as he was by her. After a few rounds of dancing, Romeo hurried over to my hiding place in the shadows.

"Isn't she beautiful, Balthasar?" he gasped. "I've never seen such a perfect face. I've never seen such a wonderful girl!"

"Yes, sir," I muttered.

"I must go and dance with her again," Romeo sighed. "I feel like a moth drawn to a flame!" He skipped away, leaving me shaking my head in disbelief. I frowned and stared at the girl Romeo was dancing with. Who was she? She was at this party, so she must be something to do with the Capulets. But then, Romeo was there, and he was no friend of the Capulets.

Suddenly, Romeo and the girl were standing close by, whispering to each other in the shadows. I couldn't hear it all but I heard enough for alarm bells to ring in my mind. When Romeo kissed her hand, I nearly jumped up to drag him out of there.

Then an old lady came and disturbed them. I guessed from her age and appearance that she was this girl's nurse.

Most children of rich families had a nurse or nanny to look after them. Sometimes, they were so loved by the families that they were kept on to serve the children when they grew up. It looked like this had happened here.

"Madam, your mother wants you," the nurse said to the girl. The girl hurried away, leaving Romeo looking embarrassed in front of the old servant.

"Tell me," Romeo asked. "Who is her mother?"

"Why Lady Capulet of course," the nurse said. "She is Juliet, the only daughter of Lord Capulet!"

I felt the blood drain from my face. How could Romeo be so stupid as to dance with Lord Capulet's daughter? And then to kiss her hand?

People were saying their goodbyes now, and the numbers in the hall thinned out to reveal Tybalt standing at the other side of the room.

Tybalt was a showoff and a bully but he wasn't a coward. He was staring at Romeo as he left and it wasn't a friendly look, either.

I ran round to the front of the house, scanning the street for Romeo but I couldn't see him. I peered into the house but all I could see was Tybalt staring out into the darkness. I shivered. He'd seen Romeo and recognised him, there was no doubt about that. What would Tybalt do about it? That was the question.

As if in answer to my thoughts, I saw Tybalt call a servant over to him. He handed a letter to the servant and muttered something. All the time he looked severe and stony faced. Whatever was in that letter, it wasn't good news for whoever received it. And I had a nasty feeling I knew who it was addressed to.

I had to warn Romeo!

I searched the crowds of partygoers walking home along the streets. Mercutio was there singing with Romeo's other friends, but there was no sign of Romeo.

Then a shadowy movement in the Capulets' orchard caught my attention and I saw him, slipping between the trees. Romeo was sneaking back into the Capulets' house!

# 4 Promises in the darkness

My heart pounded as I climbed over the orchard wall and went after Romeo. If I was caught here now, Lord Capulet's guards would kill me without hesitation. I was more worried about Romeo, though. I knew him well. He could be so foolish sometimes, especially over a beautiful girl. I had to stop him and get him back home.

Romeo was hiding in the shadows at the foot of the house wall, staring up at a balcony where Juliet gazed down. At first I thought she'd seen him but she started to speak and I realised that she was talking to herself.

"If only he wasn't a Montague," she sighed. "I wish he would give up his name or if he won't, then I'll give up mine!"

I stopped, not believing what I was hearing. Was Juliet in love with Romeo too?

But Romeo had stepped out of the shadows. "I'll gladly change my name if it means you will love me!" he declared.

Juliet almost screamed.

I wanted to rush out too and drag Romeo away but I was scared that adding to the noise might only draw more attention.

"Romeo, how did you get here? If my father's guards catch you, they'll put you to death!" Juliet said, leaning over the balcony to stare at him.

"I'd rather die here than be without your love ever again!" he cried out.

To be honest, it was a bit embarrassing listening to my best friend making such romantic statements. Maybe that was another reason I didn't jump out and stop him. I tried not to listen and concentrated on checking around the orchard for any guards who might be sneaking up on us. Nobody came.

Juliet's voice dragged my attention away from lookout duty. "I do love you but it all seems too sudden," she said. "I must go – goodnight!"

"Would you leave me so soon?" Romeo groaned. "Tell me that you love me."

"I could tell you all night," Juliet replied.

I heard a voice from inside
the house calling Juliet's name.
It sounded like the nurse.
Juliet dashed inside but came back
almost straight away. "I must be
quick, dear Romeo, but if your
intentions are honourable and
you want to marry me, then I'll
send a messenger tomorrow to
arrange it."

I didn't hear the rest. I was too
stunned. Marriage? They'd only met a few hours ago
and they were talking about marriage?

"Send the messenger at nine," Romeo called back.
"I'll have everything arranged by then!"

Surely he couldn't be serious?

The nurse called again.

Juliet said her goodbyes and ran back into her room. Before I could approach him, Romeo had vanished into the shadows. Suddenly, I was all alone in the enemy's gardens. I shivered and crept out as quickly as I could, still wondering what I should do. I thought about telling Romeo's father but couldn't bring myself to betray Romeo's trust in me. What would Romeo think of me if he found I'd been spying on him? I had to warn him about Tybalt too.

I searched the town for Romeo and returned home, tired and worried sick. Lord Montague was pacing up and down, holding a letter in his hand. I knew who the letter was from.

"Have you seen Romeo?" he asked.

"No, my Lord," I said, trying to look over Lord Montague's shoulder at the letter.

"Tybalt has challenged him to a duel!" Lord Montague spat. "Why did he have to go to the Capulets' ball?"

"I'll find him, your Lordship," I said, backing out of the room, "before Tybalt does."

I didn't find Romeo till the next morning. He was in the town square with Mercutio and Benvolio. I ran forward to warn him but the Capulets' nurse appeared with a servant. Mercutio made some comments to her and she looked very angry but Romeo said something to calm her down and walked her across the square. I knew what he was up to.

The woman hurried away and I followed Romeo to the church. I tried to catch Romeo at the door and warn him about Tybalt but he'd gone inside already. As I slipped into the cool and shade of the huge building, I heard him talking.

Friar Laurence, our local priest, stood by the altar at the far end of the church. He had a hand on Romeo's shoulder.

"Keep calm, my son," the friar said. "You charge into these things too eagerly."

"But I can't wait," Romeo said. "If I dropped down dead once we were married, it would be worth it just for the few moments of having Juliet as my wife!"

I stood in the shadows, my mouth hanging open. He was talking about his insane wedding plans to Friar Laurence. What was he thinking of? I felt a little relieved too, thinking that the friar would talk sense into him.

"I need you to be sensible," the friar said, shaking Romeo. "If you do get married, we need to keep it secret until we can find the right time to tell your parents. You might be right that the love between you and Juliet will bring the two families together. Your marriage might end this foolish feud once and for all but we have to tread carefully."

I couldn't believe it! Friar Laurence was going along with this nonsense? Did he really believe that marrying Romeo and Juliet would end the hatred between their two families? Maybe he thought it was possible, but I wasn't so sure.

"Here she is, now!" Romeo cried, running to the door to meet Juliet. I shrank deeper into the shadows as Juliet came into the church, accompanied by her nurse.

The old lady looked almost as excited as Juliet, and kept crying and dabbing her eyes with a handkerchief. She was going on about how it only seemed ten minutes ago that Juliet was a little girl and now here she was getting married. In the end, she calmed down and Friar Laurence started the wedding ceremony.

There, in the church, I watched Juliet Capulet kneel beside Romeo Montague and listened as they made their wedding vows to each other.

Meanwhile, out in the streets, Tybalt searched for Romeo, sword in hand.

# 5 The duel

The grin on Romeo's face after the marriage almost dazzled me.
I'd never seen him so happy. Friar Laurence put a hand on his
shoulder, breaking Romeo's hug with Juliet.

"And now you must show a little patience," the friar said,
smiling gently. "As soon as it's safe, you two shall be together
but before that we must all be careful."

"I don't care about
anything except my Juliet!"
Romeo exclaimed, throwing
his arms into the air.

"Nor I, my Romeo!"
Juliet laughed, hugging him.

The friar frowned and
pulled them apart again.
"All very nice," he said,
"but we must choose
the right moment to tell
your parents. Romeo, you
must go back to your house
and try to act as if nothing
has happened."

"I'll take her home before she pops with excitement!" the nurse said, leading Juliet away.

Even when Juliet had gone, Romeo kept smiling. I followed him outside and caught up with him.

"Balthasar, where did you spring from?" Romeo asked, smiling at me.

"I have a confession to make", I said, and told him everything – how I'd followed him, how I knew of his plans. "But I haven't told anyone, sir. You can trust me. I just wish you'd reconsider and tell your parents."

"Friar Laurence has a plan," Romeo said, sternly. "If I tell my father and mother now, it'll be too much of a shock for them. When the right moment comes, we'll break the happy news. But even if they don't agree, they can't keep us apart. It's too late."

"I know, sir, but …" I stopped, and my heart froze as I looked across the town square. Tybalt stood, swinging his sword and arguing with Mercutio. Beside them, Benvolio, another of Romeo's friends, looked on in dismay, trying to calm the two men down. As soon as Tybalt saw Romeo, he turned away from Mercutio and strode towards us.

"You," he called, narrowing his dark eyes and scowling at Romeo. "Draw your sword. I mean to make you pay for insulting my uncle last night!"

I held my breath. Romeo could be so unpredictable and he had a fierce temper too. Would he fight Tybalt?

Romeo raised his hands. "Tybalt, if I've upset you, I apologise," he said. I could see Mercutio's eyes widening with disbelief as he spoke. Romeo continued. "Please forgive me."

Tybalt looked confused. He glanced at Mercutio, suspecting some kind of trick perhaps, but Mercutio looked as surprised as Tybalt.

"Draw your sword, you villain!" Tybalt repeated.

Romeo just shook his head. "One day you'll understand, Tybalt, but for now, just believe me when I say that I care about the Capulets as if they were my own family."

Because they are, I thought. You've married Tybalt's cousin.

Romeo walked away across the square, leaving Tybalt looking a bit stupid just standing there with his sword in his hand and nobody to fight. But the hot weather had got to Mercutio.

"What? Are you just going to walk away?" he called after Romeo. "I never took you for such a coward."

Tybalt was still angry. "Why?" he snapped at Mercutio. "Do you want to defend his honour?" He raised his sword.

"I might just do that," Mercutio growled, drawing his own weapon.

Benvolio stepped forward. "Stop, gentlemen," he said. "The Prince has forbidden any fighting in public!"

"Who cares?" Mercutio snapped, pushing Benvolio aside. "I'm not letting this buffoon insult my friends!"

"Nobody calls me a buffoon and lives to tell the tale!" Tybalt snarled.

I stood frozen, unable to speak as Tybalt and Mercutio started
their duel. Swords clashed and glinted in the bright sunlight.
I could hear them grunting as they jabbed at each other and
leapt back, trying to trick each other into making a wrong move.

Then suddenly, Romeo appeared. "Mercutio, Tybalt, no!"
he cried, jumping between them to stop the fight. It was
a dangerous thing to do; they fought quickly, their
blades swinging and whistling through the air so fast.
Romeo could easily have been injured. It made
fighting difficult for Mercutio, though, because
he didn't want to hurt Romeo.

I watched in horror as Tybalt lunged
forward, slipping his blade under
Romeo's arm and into Mercutio's
chest. Mercutio gave a groan
and fell to the floor.

"Mercutio! Are you hurt?" Benvolio yelled, leaping to raise his friend off the ground. Mercutio looked up, and tried to laugh through the pain. "It's just a scratch," he gasped, then his smile fell into a grimace. "But it's enough. I'm dying." He glared at Romeo. "Why did you get in the way? He stabbed me under your arm!"

"I didn't want you to fight," Romeo said, horror etched on his face.

"This is your fault!" Mercutio gasped. "You Montagues and Capulets and your stupid arguments!" He fell back.

"Romeo," Benvolio whispered. "He's dead!"

Romeo said nothing but turned to face Tybalt, who stood
a few metres away. I could see the rage in Romeo's eyes.
"Draw your sword, Tybalt," he growled. "Mercutio's dead
and you or I shall join him today!"

"His death is your fault, boy!" Tybalt snapped. "He died in
your place!"

Romeo gave a roar and slashed the air with his sword.
Tybalt leapt back, stunned by Romeo's anger. I watched
helplessly as they fought. More and more people gathered
around them – Montagues, Capulets and townsfolk.

"Prepare to die, Tybalt!" Romeo snarled and lunged forward.
Tybalt smacked the blade aside and tried to stab at Romeo but
Romeo brought his sword forward, and almost by accident,
Tybalt ran on to the blade. His eyes bulged and he fell, blood
staining his jacket.

For a moment, silence filled the town square. Then the crowd began to mutter.

"Get the guard," someone said.

"Call the Prince!" another cried.

"Murder!"

Benvolio ran to Romeo and I followed. "Romeo, you must get away," he said. "The Prince said that anyone else caught fighting would pay with their life."

Romeo stared down at Tybalt's body. "Why am I such a fool?" he said. "It was never my fate to be happy!"

I grabbed Romeo's arm and dragged him away. Somewhere in the distance, a fanfare told us that the Prince was on his way.

# 6 Worse than death

Leaving Romeo in the church, I hurried back to the square.
A huge crowd had gathered around the Prince, who sat on his
horse looking down at the bodies of Mercutio and Tybalt.
People were shouting for Romeo to be executed and others
were begging the Prince to be merciful.

Finally, Lord Montague spoke and the crowd fell silent.
"My Prince," he said. "My son only did what the law
demanded. Tybalt killed Mercutio and so Romeo killed Tybalt.
Wouldn't you have done the same?"

Lord Capulet stepped forward. "That's nonsense,
your Highness!" he yelled. "Tybalt was my nephew. Romeo
deserves to die!"

The Prince silenced him with a flick of his hand. He stared down, sadly, at the fallen Mercutio. "I have lost a kinsman, today, too, Montague," the Prince said, quietly. "And there has been enough killing." He raised his hand. "Romeo is banished from this land! He must remove himself from Verona and never return. If he's seen within these city walls, he'll be executed. These are my final words on the matter!"

With a flourish of trumpets, the Prince wheeled his horse around and trotted out of the square, followed by his guards and several townsfolk.

I hurried back to the church but Friar Laurence was there before me. I reached them just in time to hear him delivering the news to Romeo.

His voice was low and steady. "You've been banished from Verona …"

But Romeo let out a cry of agony. "Then I may as well be dead!"

The friar was furious at Romeo's reaction to the news. "Look at you!" the priest said, shaking Romeo. "Bawling and crying like a toddler, kicking the floor and the pews. It could have been a lot worse!"

"Didn't you hear him? I'm banished! Exiled. I'll never see Juliet again!" Romeo sobbed. "How could it have been worse?"

Friar Laurence threw up his hands. "You could have been executed!" he bellowed, making me flinch.

The priest calmed himself, straightening his robes. He lowered his voice but I could tell he was struggling to keep his temper with Romeo. "You're alive, you're lucky. Now," he said, "you go to Mantua, the next town along the road from here, and wait there. When the time is right, we can still break the news and Juliet can come and join you. This will all blow over."

"As long as I can be with my beloved Juliet," Romeo sniffled, wiping his eyes. "I'd rather be dead than without her."

I shook my head but kept quiet. Romeo was like a man obsessed. What about his mother and father? They must be worried sick and heartbroken too but he didn't spare a thought for them. What about poor Mercutio lying dead in the street? I have to admit that I didn't really like Romeo at that point. He seemed so selfish.

The church door creaked open, making us all jump, but it was only Juliet's servant, the nurse. Her eyes were red with crying.

"How is my Lady Juliet?" Romeo demanded, leaping forward. "Does she think I'm an evil murderer?"

The woman shook her head. "She doesn't know what to think," she said. "One minute she calls Tybalt's name, the next yours."

"It's all my fault," Romeo sobbed. "I've made her so miserable!"

"She asked me to give you this," the nurse said, pulling a ring from her bag. "She said to say goodbye before you leave. Somehow she'll join you when the time's right."

It was dark by the time Romeo came out of the church. He disguised himself and sneaked into the Capulets' orchard once more to say goodbye to Juliet while I went to fetch some horses to carry him and his belongings.

I sighed as I led the animals, laden with bags and boxes, back to the edge of town. I didn't like Mercutio or Tybalt but they hadn't deserved to die. I was angry with Romeo too, for being so selfish. At least Juliet would be able to join him at some point, I thought. Maybe some good would come out of all this. Maybe the two families would be united at last. Romeo finally arrived and I waved him off in the gathering dawn with a heavy heart but a feeling that things could only get better.

Little did I know they were about to take a turn for the worse.

# 7 A tangled web

The last thing that Romeo said to me before he left was,
"Keep an eye on Juliet, Balthasar. You're my loyal servant.
Send me news if you're worried about anything."

I frowned at that. "I will, sir," I said. "But what could possibly
happen? Things will calm down again, you'll see. Eventually,
the Prince will forgive you. He might even do it soon, if he
discovers that you and Juliet are married and the families united!"

Romeo sighed and gave me a sad smile. "I hope you're right,
Balthasar," he said, patting my shoulder. "But I feel as if I'll never
see my Juliet again."

I watched as Romeo rode out of town towards
Mantua, his new home. He needn't be so glum,
I thought. Things will improve!

I was thinking this as I wandered past the Capulets' house. The sound of raised voices and screaming blew my reassuring daydreams into the gutter. A servant hurried out of the front door, looking flustered.

"What's happened?" I called after him.

The man stopped; he looked in a state of shock. I'm sure he wouldn't normally share such private information but he'd obviously been shaken and so he forgot himself. "Lord Capulet, thinking he would end all this bad news with some good, has agreed that Paris, the Prince's cousin, can marry Juliet."

"No!" I gasped.

"Yes!" The man replied, encouraged by my horror but not knowing the real truth. "Juliet refused. She started screaming and bawling at him. Lord Capulet is sending her to Friar Laurence to get him to talk sense into her. It was a terrible scene!"

I wasn't listening though; I was running to the church. Juliet couldn't possibly marry Paris. She was married already! Apart from Romeo and Juliet, nobody knew that, except me, the friar and the nurse. What should I do?

If I went after Romeo, he'd come back to certain death.
If I did nothing, then would the wedding go ahead? If Juliet
refused, would she be thrown out of her father's house?
Capulet was a fierce man and daughters were expected to obey
their fathers even when it came to choosing a husband.
Juliet was very brave to stand up to him.

I burst into the church, searching the vestry and cells at
the back. Then looking through a window, I saw Friar Laurence
out in the churchyard talking to Paris. I heaved a sigh of relief.

He was deep in conversation, shaking his head and Paris
looked crestfallen. Maybe the friar had talked him out of
the idea of marriage!

Then Juliet appeared at the gate. Friar Laurence brought her into the church and I sneaked out. Juliet didn't really know me and might not trust me, especially if she caught me eavesdropping on her conversation with the friar.

I just caught part of the priest's conversation with her. "Don't worry, my dear, I have a plan," he said.

I felt a little easier. It sounded as if Friar Laurence had everything under control. I wondered if I should tell Romeo about what had happened but then decided against it. Looking back, I suppose if I had, then perhaps he'd have come back, the truth would have been told and everything would've been all right but that's not what I did and not what happened.

The news of Juliet and Paris's hasty wedding spread across town like wildfire. It couldn't be hidden. Servants were running around buying up the finest food and linen for the tables, flowers were being arranged in the church. I began to worry.

What was Friar Laurence up to? Was Juliet being forced to marry Paris? I paced around town, unable to think about my duties. All day I watched the church closely, trying to guess at the friar's plan but it couldn't work out.

As dusk fell, I crept into the Capulets' orchard once again and tried to see into the house. It was dangerous but I had to find out what was going on. Peering through an open window, all I could see were servants bustling about, sweeping and setting tables ready for the big day. Lord Capulet strode around, pointing out things that needed doing.

I saw Juliet once but she seemed happy and calm. A horrible thought crossed my mind. Was she planning to betray Romeo? He was miles away and couldn't come back. Who'd blame her for ditching him for a man like Paris? He was rich and handsome, and related to the Prince. Romeo wouldn't dare come causing trouble. And who'd believe him anyway? But deep down, I was certain Juliet wouldn't betray Romeo. She was in love with him!

I still needed to find out what was going on, so I took another chance and hid in the tree close to Juliet's balcony. Maybe if I overheard some conversation from the balcony or Juliet's room, I'd find out more. I wondered again whether I should go to Mantua and tell Romeo.

The night felt warm and I had been worrying and creeping around all day. I didn't mean to but at some point I must have dozed off because the next thing I knew it was morning and someone was screaming in horror!

# 8 Shock news!

It was a wonder I didn't fall out of the tree because the scream was so blood-curdling! From my hiding place, I could see into Juliet's room.

The nurse knelt at the foot of the bed as if saying her prayers, Lord and Lady Capulet held each other and looked down at the still form lying there.

Juliet lay asleep on the bed, her arms folded across her chest. Then Lady Capulet cried, "My child! My daughter is dead!"

My heart pounded and I felt dizzy as I tried to take in the scene and make sense of it. How could she be dead? She was so young! She had her whole life ahead of her. A life with Romeo. I swallowed back tears. She seemed a sweet girl and this was too much to bear.

Now I could hear people weeping – servants, family members. They were full of joyful bustle yesterday and suddenly a second tragedy had struck this family. First Tybalt, now Juliet!

Was this Friar Laurence's plan? Surely not! He'd never tell Juliet to kill herself. Maybe the situation was just too hard for her and she took her own life. Or maybe she just got ill overnight and died. I'd heard of that happening before now.

I shivered in the cool of the morning. I'd have to go and tell Romeo. But how would he react?

Slipping down from the tree, I crept out of the orchard. If anyone saw me, they didn't make any comment. Everyone was so heartbroken that Juliet had died.

I hurried back to the church to see if I could talk to Friar Laurence but he was busy talking to members of the Capulets' household. The wedding flowers that had filled the church only a few hours ago were discarded and replaced with funeral wreaths. I waited and waited, hoping to get a chance to speak to the friar but he disappeared into his cell and then I couldn't find him.

Pretty soon, it was time for the funeral and I watched as Juliet's body was brought out on a stretcher strewn with flowers.

61

Friar Laurence walked at the head of the procession reading prayers out loud, and the Capulets followed. Poor old Paris stumbled along looking stunned and confused. I felt sorry for him. One day he was getting ready to be a bridegroom, the next, he was at his bride's funeral.

The Capulets had a huge mausoleum, a big marble building where they laid their dead. Its iron gates hung open, waiting for the procession.

As they went in, I couldn't bear it any longer. I ran from the graveyard and grabbed my horse. I had to tell Romeo. But what he would do when he heard the news, I dreaded to think!

# 9 The messenger

The journey to Mantua was probably the worst of my life.
I wanted to turn back. I didn't want to be the one to tell Romeo
that Juliet was dead. What if he flew into a rage and killed me?
What if he hurt himself? I tried to think of ways to tell him that
wouldn't sound so bad but none of them worked. The only way
was to tell him straight.

I found Romeo roaming the streets of Mantua not far from
the rooms where he was staying. He hugged me like a long-lost
brother and my heart ached with the message I had to deliver.

"How is my Lady Juliet?" he said, a smile breaking his weary-looking face for a moment.

I couldn't think of any other way to tell him. "She's …
dead … sir. I have just come from her funeral."

Romeo looked pale as I explained what had happened.
He sat listening in silence, as still as a statue. His eyes glistened
with tears but otherwise it looked as if the news had frozen him
to ice. When I'd finished he stood up. He wiped his eyes with
the sleeve of his jacket and heaved an enormous, sobbing sigh.
Then he shook himself and stood up straight.

"Get the horses," he said. "I'm going back to Verona."

I hesitated. I'd never seen Romeo like this before. "Are you sure, sir, you look so pale," I said. "I'm frightened you'll do something terrible …"

Romeo took a breath. He was trying to control himself but he looked as if he could explode at any minute. "Nonsense," he said, but I could hear his voice was on the verge of breaking up. "I'm fine. Do as I say. I want to go and pay my last respects. Are you sure there wasn't any word from Friar Laurence? No letters?"

I shook my head and left.

I should've guessed he was up to something then. He seemed so falsely calm as if he was struggling to control himself. As I went to fetch the horses, I looked over my shoulder to see him disappearing into a shabby-looking shop.

I brought the horses around but before we left, Romeo wrote a letter and sealed it. He sent me off to buy a spade and a crowbar too. My heart filled with dread. What possible use could he have for such tools? What madness was he planning?

We galloped all the way back to Verona. Romeo barely said a word and we didn't pause for rest, food or water. By the time we reached the graveyard in Verona, it was growing dark. Romeo dismounted and took the letter he'd written.

"Here," he said, passing the letter to me. "Take this to my father and mother ..."

"But what are you going to do?" I said.

Romeo put a hand on my shoulder. "Don't worry, I just want to take a last look at my lady's face, that's all," he said. His face hardened. "Now you go home and don't come back. If I see you here again, you'll be in big trouble! Good luck, my friend. We'll not meet again."

He took the spade and the crowbar and hurried off into
the night. My heart pounded. He'd told me to leave. He was
my master but I was frightened he was going to do
something terrible.

I didn't know what to do. I crouched behind a gravestone
and watched as Romeo used the spade and the crowbar to
break into the mausoleum. I shivered, thinking of all the dead
bodies down there but I was frightened too of someone coming
along and catching him. What would they think he was up to?

Romeo disappeared inside the Capulets' mausoleum. I could hear him talking to Juliet as if she was still alive but I couldn't make out the words. I crept closer but it had gone quiet. My head started to throb. If Romeo came out now and caught me skulking around the mausoleum, he'd be furious. He'd kill me, that's for sure! But I was worried.

And then a footstep behind me made me jump. A voice cried out. "Who's there?"

We'd been found out!

# 10 Disaster!

I turned to see who approached. I could hardly breathe as I stared into the darkness. I gave a huge sigh of relief as I saw the worried features of Friar Laurence.

"It is I, Balthasar," I said.

Friar Laurence didn't look pleased to see me. "Who's down there?" he demanded.

"My master, Romeo," I replied. "He says he's paying his last respects but I'm worried about him …"

"Last respects …?" The friar went pale. "You told him Juliet was dead?"

"Yes, Father," I said. "And he looked so desperate and dangerous. I've never seen him like that before. He sent me away. He said there'd be trouble if I came back. I daren't go in!"

"Didn't he get my letter?" Friar Laurence grabbed my jacket.

"What letter?" I stammered. I felt weak at the knees. "My master, Romeo has only heard news from me. What's going on?"

"Juliet isn't dead. I merely gave her a potion to make her seem like she was dead," the friar said, glancing into the mausoleum.

"I was to wake her up at this time and bring her
to Mantua to be with Romeo. I sent Romeo a letter explaining
all this but it seems it didn't get to him." His eyes widened.
"But if Romeo thinks Juliet is dead ... oh no! Oh no!"

Friar Laurence hurried through the metal doors of
the mausoleum and down the steps. I stood shivering at the top.
Finally, I plucked up the courage to go down a few of the steps.

I gasped in horror and wonder at the sight. My master lay dead on the floor, a small bottle of poison by his side.

Friar Laurence knelt beside Juliet, shaking her. Slowly she was beginning to wake up. She yawned and stretched as if she'd just woken from a good night's sleep.

"Is it time?" she said in a croaky voice. "Where's my husband?"

Friar Laurence trembled. "It's too late, girl, your husband is dead," he said. "Come with me now. I'll make sure you're safe."

But Juliet ignored him and stared down at Romeo.

From where I stood I could tell that Juliet wasn't going to leave him. I heard a sound from above us in the graveyard. More footsteps!

"We must go, before we're caught!" Friar Laurence pleaded.

"You go," Juliet said, calmly. "I'm not leaving Romeo."

"I can't stay any longer!" Friar Laurence yelled. "I'm sorry, Juliet. I didn't mean any harm!" He ran past me, almost knocking me down into the mausoleum.

I didn't know what to do. My master lay dead on the floor and Juliet didn't know me so I couldn't reason with her. I ran up to the graveyard for help. Two night watchmen appeared from the darkness.

"You've got to come quickly!" I said. "To where Lady Juliet lies."

The watchmen followed me through the gravestones and down into the mausoleum. It echoed with our cries as we found Lady Juliet wrapped in Romeo's arms and a dagger through her heart.

Juliet was dead.

# 11 A new peace

The people of Verona crowded around the market square and
I stood next to Friar Laurence, hanging my head in shame.
The Prince sat on a throne that had been brought out into
the open so that all could hear the story.

"I thought the marriage of Romeo and Juliet would unite
the two families and they would put aside their hatred,"
Friar Laurence said, sadly.

"A noble ambition, friar, but we've all been hurt by
your actions," the Prince declared. He then turned to me.

"And you, boy?" he said. "What have you to say
for yourself?"

I felt my face flush red
and my throat went dry.
"I wish I'd stopped him,
your Highness – I feel
responsible." I handed
the Prince Romeo's letter
– the one he'd written to
his parents explaining how
he'd married his love, Juliet,
and why he couldn't live
without her.

He opened it and read it to himself. "The letter confirms the friar's story," the Prince said. He turned and faced Lord Montague and Lord Capulet. "You see what this ridiculous feud has led to? Can you see the harm it's done? We've all been punished for letting it go on for so long!"

Lord Capulet turned to Lord Montague. "Give me your hand, Brother Montague," he said. "For my daughter's sake, let this argument end."

"I'll raise a statue of pure gold in memory of your loyal and beloved daughter, Brother Capulet!" Lord Montague gripped Lord Capulet's hand.

"We'll build a memorial to both of them!" Lord Capulet said. "To Romeo and Juliet!"

And so now Verona is a peaceful, if sad, town. Life goes on and I still serve the Montagues. I can't help wishing I'd done more though. Wishing I'd not taken the message of Juliet's death. Wishing I'd stopped Romeo even meeting Juliet.
Friar Laurence says it was all bound to happen, that it was fate. But that doesn't help. I'll never forget those terrible few days when I lost my good friend and master Romeo and his true love Juliet.

# Life, love and death in Verona

It was a full-scale riot!

"I feel like a moth drawn to a flame!"

"Give me your hand."

Juliet was dead.

My master lay dead on the floor.

"I do love you."

wedding vows

"It's just a scratch.
But it's enough."

"Prepare to die, Tybalt!"

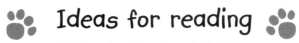

# Ideas for reading

Written by Clare Dowdall, PhD

*Lecturer and Primary Literacy Consultant*

**Reading objectives:**

- identify and discuss themes and conventions
- draw inferences such as characters' feelings, thoughts and motives from their actions, and justify inferences with evidence
- predict what might happen from details stated and implied
- discuss and evaluate how authors use language, including figurative language, considering the impact on the reader

**Spoken language objectives:**

- participate in discussions, presentations, performances, role play, improvisations and debates

**Curriculum links:** PSHE

Resources: art materials for mask-making; ICT; the Prologue from *Romeo and Juliet* (Shakespeare)

## Build a context for reading

- Ask children to share what they know already about the story of Romeo and Juliet. Introduce some key information, e.g. it is a play written by William Shakespeare; it is a tragedy, etc.
- Look at the front cover and read the blurb. Explain that this is a retelling of the play by a manservant called Balthasar.
- Look at the cast list on pp2–3, and read the names. Explain that the characters are divided into two groups of family and friends, who are enemies.

## Understand and apply reading strategies

- Read the prologue on p4. Explain that this is an introduction. Ask children to discuss the tone that Balthasar is setting, and what "all the troubles" might refer to. Consider how the author creates a tone of regret and sadness in the prologue.